WILD AMERICA
HABITATS

DESERTS

By Melissa Cole

BLACKBIRCH®
PRESS

THOMSON

GALE

San Diego • Detroit • New York • San Francisco • Cleveland • New Haven, Conn. • Waterville, Maine • London • Munich

For more information, contact
The Gale Group, Inc.
27500 Drake Rd.
Farmington Hills, MI 48331-3535
Or you can visit our Internet site at http://www.gale.com

Photo Credits: Cover, all photos © Tom and Pat Leeson Wildlife Photography; pages 19, 23 illustrations by Chris Jouan Illustration

LIBRARY OF CONGRESS CATALOGING-IN-PUBLICATION DATA

Cole, Melissa S.
    Deserts / by Melissa S. Cole.
        p. cm. — (Wild America habitats)
Contents: Climate — How do animals and plants survive in deserts? — Coping with temperature — Humans and deserts.
        ISBN 1-56711-799-6 (hardback : alk. paper)
1. Desert ecology—Juvenile literature.   [1. Deserts. 2. Desert ecology. 3. Ecology.]
I. Title. II. Series: Wild America habitats series.
QH541.5.D4C65 2003
577.54—dc21   2002012880

Printed in China
10 9 8 7 6 5 4 3 2 1

Contents

Introduction

Deserts are usually hot and dry with very little visible vegetation. The weather is extreme, with soaring daytime heat and sometimes freezing nighttime temperatures. Plants and animals have adapted to living in this challenging habitat, or type of environment.

To be considered a desert, a habitat must receive less than 10 inches (25 cm) of rain per year. The deserts in North America are varied in appearances.

Some deserts are brown and barren. Others are colorful and rocky. Each desert has a unique landscape. This kind of habitat has many hardy creatures and strong plants within its environment.

Barrel cacti bloom best in extreme desert climates.

Where Are Deserts Found Today?

North American deserts stretch from Idaho to Mexico City. They cover more than 493,000 square miles (1,276,870 square km) and are broken into four regions— the Great Basin, the Mojave, the Sonoran, and the Chihuahuan Deserts.

Most of the North American desert lies between the Sierra Nevada Range in California and the Rocky Mountains in Colorado. This area has many small mountain ranges with gently curving basins or valleys in between. When it rains, shallow lakes form in these basins. They quickly evaporate (lose water) in the heat, and leave salt flats. North American deserts do not have many sandy areas. They are mostly made up of cliffs, plateaus (large, flat, elevated pieces of land), and unusual rock formations.

Arizona's Sonoran Desert is made up of both mountains and valleys.

What Makes Deserts Unique?

Deserts vary in geography and size. Some deserts have huge canyons and mountain ranges, while others are flat and sandy. Deserts may be barren or overrun with brush and cacti. What makes all deserts unique, though, is their climate.

Most North American deserts are rocky, not sandy. Sand dunes make the desert in Eureka Valley, California, unique.

Climate

Most habitats, such as forests, have high humidity or water vapor in the air. This water reflects and absorbs the sun's energy. That keeps much of the heat generated by the sun from reaching the ground. The air in a desert is dry, though, so water vapor or clouds usually do not form. There-fore, the sun beats directly on the unprotected land. Ground temperatures can reach higher than 165°F (74°C) during the summer!

The sun can heat the unprotected desert ground to more than 165°F (74°C) in the summer.

7

The average yearly temperature in North American deserts is between 75°F (24°C) and 86°F (30°C). Death Valley, which is in the Mojave Desert, sometimes reaches temperatures above 130°F (54°C). At night, air temperatures can drop dramatically and dip down below freezing. The Sonoran Desert in southwest Arizona occasionally gets snow in winter.

Deserts are very dry, and some experience high winds. This causes dust to kick up. It can be difficult to breathe or to see because the air is a mass of drifting, swirling dust. Sometimes more dangerous storms develop. Thunderstorms are often sudden and result in flash floods. The dry, sun baked soil is unable to soak up water fast enough. This causes rain to collect on the ground's surface. It rushes over the desert floor and flows into dry desert washes, called arroyos.

Dry desert soil cannot soak up rain quickly, which can lead to flash floods. **Inset, left:** Water collects in arroyos during rainstorms. **Inset, right:** Dangerous desert thunderstorms can develop suddenly.

Coping with Temperature

Many desert animals burrow underground to escape the scorching midday heat. While the soil may reach temperatures above 165°F (74°C), underground dens remain at 80°F (27°C) or below. Burrows also trap tiny drops of moisture when animals breathe out. The moisture helps to keep them cool.

Many lizards have long toes and fringed growths on their back feet. This keeps them from sinking in hot sand. They often run upright to keep their bodies and front feet off of the hot ground. Other lizards change colors throughout the day. In the morning when it is cool, they have dark skin. This soaks up the sun's rays and warms them. As they heat up, their skin becomes lighter in color. Light skin reflects the rays of the sun and keeps them from getting too hot.

Iguanas and other small desert animals live in burrows. **Inset:** Light skin helps prevent lizards from getting too hot.

How Do Plants Survive in Deserts?

Desert plants are able to survive extreme temperatures and lack of water. Cacti and shrubs are the most common plants to do well in such conditions. Cacti and other desert plants store large amounts of water in their roots, stems, and leaves. These kinds of plants are called succulents. One succulent, the saguaro cactus swells during rainy periods. It sucks up enough water during this time to survive long periods with no rain. In fact, it can hold over 6 tons (6,096 kg) of water in its trunk!

Certain types of cacti grow in different desert regions. For example, pincushion-shaped cacti grow in the Mojave. The Sonoran Desert, which gets more rain, is home to 25-foot (7.6 m) tall saguaro cacti.

A saguaro cactus can grow to be 25 feet (7.6 m) tall, and it can hold up to 6 tons (6,096 kg) of water in its trunk.

Other types of cacti, such as prickly pear, jumping cholla, pig's ears, and organ pipe cacti can also be found in various North American deserts.

Cacti do well in deserts because of their ability to contain enough water to survive. Cacti collect energy from the sun through their thick stems. The surface of these stems is coated with a waxy substance. This prevents water loss. Many desert plants have deep pores, called stomates, that only open at night when temperatures are cooler and evaporation occurs at a slower rate.

Top: Cacti such as the cholla have wax-coated stems to prevent water loss.
Bottom: Saguaro and other cacti are covered with sharp spines.

13

Small shrubs, such as mesquite and sage, can be found in most North American deserts. Some trees and shrubs, such as cottonwoods and junipers are often able to survive along desert washes. Grasses and a few wildflowers, such as evening primrose and sego lilies, are also parts of the desert scenery.

Desert plants may appear small, but their underground root systems can be over 10 times larger than what is visible above ground. Some plants have shallow roots that spread out under the soil's surface. This allows them to soak up water from a quick rain—or even from morning dew.

Wildflowers such as sand verbenas (top) and desert lilies (bottom) grow in many North American deserts.

Other plants have long roots called taproots that absorb water from underground sources. A mesquite's taproot can grow to be more than 100 feet (30 m) long!

Plants often grow with a lot of space around them. This is because many plants release chemicals into the soil to prevent other plants from growing too close. This ensures that each plant has enough water and soil nutrients in its own area.

Mesquite trees and shrubs grow along desert washes.

How Do Animals Survive in Deserts?

Two-thirds of animals that live in deserts are small rodents such as pocket mice, kangaroo rats, and pack rats. These animals feed mainly on seeds. Animals also get most of their water from seeds, which are made up of 20 to 50 percent water. Rodents store food in burrows for times of drought or in case it snows in winter. Burrows also allow small animals to hide from predators such as coyotes, kit foxes, and owls. Pack rats often build burrows under clumps of prickly pear cactus. The spines on this cactus protect them from their enemies—and pack rats eat the prickly pear fruit.

The bird population in deserts varies with the time of year. Some birds, such as the cactus wren and Gambel's quail, are able to withstand the heat and find food all year long. Other birds migrate to places with milder climates when the weather becomes too hot or too cold.

Cactus wrens are able to find food in the desert all year long.

Because there are so few trees in deserts, birds often build nests in the thorny branches of shrubs and cacti. There are plenty of insects and scorpions for birds and other predators to feed on.

Predators, such as Gila monsters and western diamondback rattlesnakes, do well in the desert. They feed on insects and small rodents. Many of these animals are poisonous. They wait for their prey, then kill them with a quick, venomous bite. Many animals feed at night when it is cooler. Coyotes and kit foxes sleep in rocky caves during the day. At night they search for insects, lizards, and snakes to eat. Mountain lions—also known as cougars or pumas—roam the high desert. They prey on deer, big-horn sheep, and antelope.

Western diamondback rattlesnakes blend in with the desert floor.

Food Chain

All living creatures need energy to live. Energy is transferred from one living thing to another through food and sunlight. For example, plants use sunlight to make sugar. This becomes energy for plants. Sugar is then stored in the plant's leaves, shoots, roots, and seeds. When an insect eats a plant, some of the plant's energy becomes part of it. Energy is passed from creature to creature through feeding. Scavengers such as turkey vultures and insects eat what is left of a dead animal. Decomposers such as fungi and bacteria breakdown the last bits. Any leftovers become part of the soil. Roots absorb nutrition from the soil in addition to the energy that their leaves receive from the sun. Then the whole cycle begins again. This process of energy passing between organisms as they feed upon one another is called a food chain.

Vultures are among the last animals to feed in the food chain.

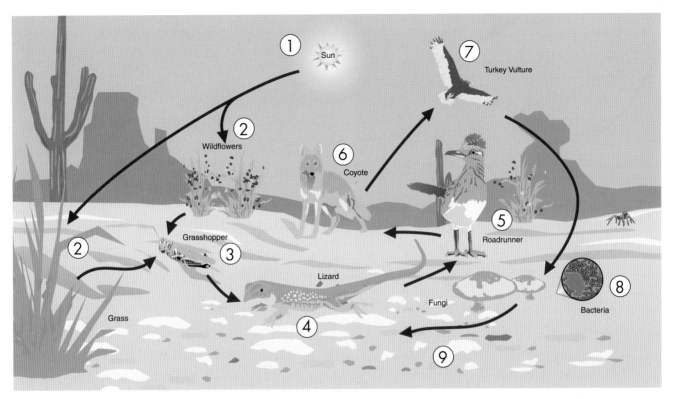

The food chain shows a step-by-step example of how energy in the desert is exchanged through food: The sun (1) is the first source of energy for all living things on earth. Green plants such as grasses and wildflowers (2) are able to use sunlight and carbon dioxide in the air to create sugar, which the plants use as food. The grasses are then eaten for food by the grasshopper (3), which in turn is caught and eaten by the lizard (4). The roadrunner (5) eats the lizard and is then itself caught and eaten by the coyote (6). When the coyote dies, the turkey vulture eats its dead body. When the vulture dies and falls to the ground, worms, fungi, bacteria (7), and other decomposers feed on its body. Finally, these creatures or their waste products end up as soil nutrients (8), which are then taken up by the roots of the pine trees as part of their nourishment. The cycle then repeats.

Humans and Deserts

Desert areas have some of the most rapid population growth in the United States. Many acres of desert habitat are lost because land is being cleared and developed for homes, shopping centers, and businesses.

One of the biggest problems this habitat faces is the overuse of desert water. In the deserts that surround Las Vegas and Phoenix, acres of land are cleared and irrigated for golf courses. So much water is pumped out of the Colorado River that by the time it reaches Mexico, it is barely more than a stream. Overuse of water also lowers underground water levels. When this happens, plants' taproots cannot get to the water they need.

In places like Tucson, Arizona, many acres of desert land have been cleared to make room for communities.

Water is also used to irrigate crops in the desert. Water evaporates quickly in the hot climate, so much of it is wasted. As water flows over ground, it picks up fertilizers and insecticides as well as naturally occurring chemicals from the soil. When the water evaporates, it leaves these chemicals on the soil. The soil becomes so salty and polluted that crops will not grow in it. Farmers then clear new areas of desert to grow their crops.

Soil erosion—the loss of nutrient-rich topsoil—also affects the desert. Off-road vehicles used by people for recreation kill plants and grasses. When this happens, plants' roots can no longer hold topsoil in place. Grazing cattle also contribute to soil erosion. Cows trample grass and overgraze fragile plants, which leaves soil dry and dusty. Farmers are forced to move their cattle to new desert patches to graze.

People who live in Las Vegas are concerned with the government's decision to locate the nation's first long-term storage site for spent nuclear fuel and high level radioactive waste in Nevada. This land includes Yucca Mountain, and is located one hundred miles northwest of Las Vegas in the middle of the Western Shoshone Reservation. The government plans to bury 17,000 tons of nuclear waste at this site. People worry that nuclear waste will leak into the ground or water sources and pollute the environment and increase rates of cancer in humans.

How Humans Can Preserve Desert Habitats

Although the desert faces many challenges to its existence, there are several things that people can do to help preserve it. The government can continue to set aside and preserve large areas of desert.If people work hard to protect and preserve desert areas, then this habitat has a chance to survive.

Some desert areas, such as Joshua Tree National Park, are protected by the government from development.

A Desert's Food Web

Food webs show how creatures in a habitat depend on one another to survive. Yellow arrows: creatures nourished by the sun; Green arrows: animals and insects that eat green plants; Orange arrows: predators; Red arrows: scavengers and decomposers. The energy then returns to the soil and is taken up by green plants, and the cycle repeats.

Glossary

Arroyos Dry stream beds with steep banks; arroyos carry water deposited by desert rains

Adapt To change a behavior or characteristic so as to increase the chance of survival in a particular habitat

Burrow A hole in the ground made by an animal for shelter

Decomposers Animals, such as earthworms, and plants, such as fungi, that eat dead tissue and return nutrients to the soil

Desert A region that receives less than 10 inches (25 cm) of rain annually

Food Chain The process of energy passing between organisms as they feed upon one another.

Food Web A series of food chains that are linked together to show the sequence of plants and animals that depend on one another for food within an ecosystem

Habitat The area in which a plant or animal naturally lives. Habitats provide living organisms with everything they need to survive— food, water, and shelter.

Humidity The amount of water vapor present in the air

Plateau A flat highland

Predators Animals, such as cougars, that hunt other animals for food

Preserve A place where habitat is protected from development. Plants and animals are allowed to live in their natural habitat without people.

Prey An animal killed and eaten by another animal

Rodents Plant-eating mammals that gnaw with their teeth

Scavengers Animals, such as ravens, that feed on dead animals

Succulents Plants that can store large amounts of water

For Further Reading

Books

Arnold, Caroline. *Watching Desert Wildlife*. Minneapolis: Carolrhoda, 1994.

Moore, Randy. *Living Desert*. Berkeley Heights, NJ: Enslow, 1991.

Sayre, April Pulley. *Deserts*. New York: Twenty-First Century Books, 1994.

Twist, Clint. *Ecology Watch, Deserts*. New York: Dillon Press, 1991.

Watts, Barrie. *24 Hours in a Desert*. New York: Franklin Watts, 1991.

Web sites

Kofa Wildlife Refuge site **http://www.fws.gov**

Organ Pipe Cactus National Monument site **http://www.nps.gov/orpi**

Mojave Desert site **http://www.desertusa.com/du_mojave.html**

Index